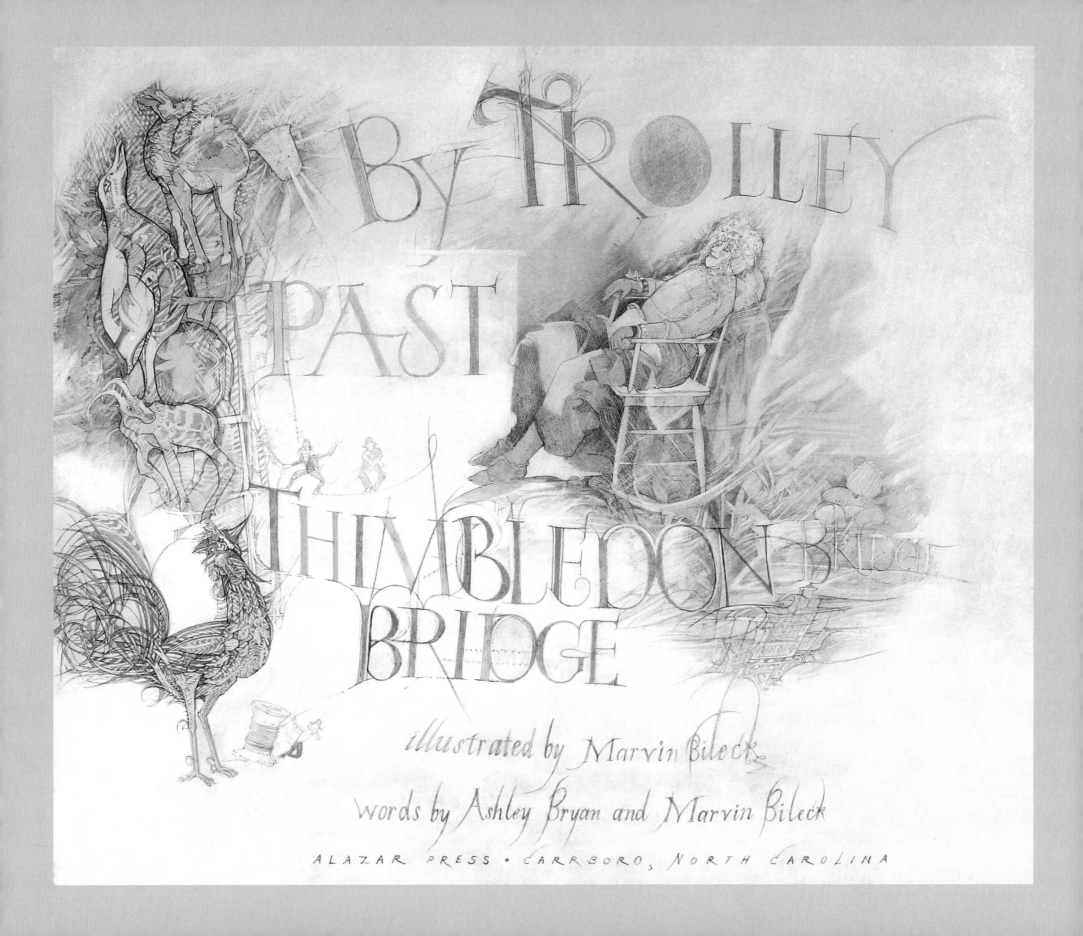

By Trolley Past Thimbledon Bridge

illustrated by Marvin Bileck

words by Ashley Bryan and Marvin Bileck

ALAZAR PRESS · CARRBORO, NORTH CAROLINA

OUR DAY-DREAMS AND FANCIES
TAKE OFF IN OUR PLAY
WHAT'S REAL, WHATS IMAGINED
NO ONE CAN SAY.

FOR, DEAR EMILY WHO OPENS DOORS

NURSE
R-Y
RHYME

The Story Behind The Story

Buddy was delighted when the Virginia Woolf Estate contacted him about doing the illustrations for the only children's story Virginia Woolf ever wrote. He began work at once. But it took much longer than anticipated and the Estate withdrew its contract leaving Buddy with pages of illustrations but no text. He was heartbroken. When he told his friend Ashley Bryan, they began playfully bantering back and forth with words here and there, in and out of the drawings, and that's how *By Trolley Past Thimbledon Bridge* came into being.

Emily Nelligan Bileck

Knowing how tirelessly my friend, Buddy, worked on the illustrations for over ten years, I offered him my help in creating a new text. Since the late 1970's I have made efforts to have this book put into production. I wish to share Buddy's extraordinary visual adventures with a vast world of viewers. I am happy to know that Alazar Press will be the one to offer Buddy's work to a wide audience.

Ashley Bryan

Until her official retirement in 1985, Jean Karl was the renowned children's editor at Atheneum Books. She continued to serve as an editor-at-large until shortly before her death in 2000. It was Jean who opened the publishing doors for the now legendary author and illustrator, Ashley Bryan. When the Virginia Woolf text was withdrawn from the illustrations of Marvin Bileck, Ashley knew to turn to Jean to guide the project that would pair Ashley and Marvin to create the new text. Ashley could not bear to think that ten years of Marvin's extraordinary work would be wasted. They had been friends since the early 1940's after meeting at The Cooper Union, a privately funded college in New York City, in the School of Art.

Still, this book has remained a work in progress for decades. It has patiently waited for its moment. On February 15, 1977, Jean Karl wrote a letter to Ashley Bryan: "I am delighted that you and Marvin Bileck are coming along so well on the text of *By Trolley Past Thimbledon Bridge*. I have great hopes for that book. I think it can become a classic." Jean guided the text of Ashley and his Buddy. Finally, its time has come and Alazar Press is honored to be a part of the story of this book. The real story behind the story is one of friendship.

Rosemarie Gulla, Alazar Press

THIMBLEDON BRIDGE

Thimbledon Bridge is a merry mile long.
No one can cross who is cross.
It boasts a moon quite enormously blown
By bubble-man, bassoonist, Peat Moss.

People cross on the hour.
They rock the bell tower
That clangs by the shimmering sea.

They pay the play price,
As they sing in deep voice
To giraffe who collects the fee.

"If our tower should tumble,
The bridge too would crumble
And splash in our Sassafras Tea.
Ah me!"

Skip aboard children,
Hurry if you can.
Trolley's now leaving
For Thimbledon Land.

Our day-dreams and fancies
Take off in our play.
What's real, what's imagined,
No one can say.

It won't cost a penny
It won't cost a dime
All in together now
We leave on time.

We'll rock on the bridge
Along Trolley Line Lane.
We'll fish, stitch and picnic
And dance in the rain.

Sew a stitch
Cast a line
Catch your fish
And I'll catch mine.

Sink the needle
Into the blue,
Draw out rabbits,
Baby-doe, too.

My cloth works magic
And like a pool
Reflects all images
Reeled from my spool.

Stories in my head,
Fishes in my pail,
One stitch, two stitch
Catch'em by the tail.

*S*eek no further.
Marry me
Meandering maid
In my apple tree.

I think I know
Just where we are.
We're half-way under
The morning star.

Roll along trolley
Ding, ring the bell, Dong!
Here's Antelope Station,
Is everyone on?

The journey's as silent
As snowfalls at night.
Folks think we're nearby
But we've slipped out of sight.

We transfer by ferry
Round Ride-A-Way Place
Where Wee Mouse and Long Hare
Get set for a race.

One for the money, two for the show
Teddy sings "ready!"
Goat cries "GO!"

*W*inds blow east
Winds blow west
Branches tangle
Billows crest.

Cat's at the window
Ostrich in the glade
Elephant and zebra,
Giraffe parade.

Tiger tiptoes
To Timbuctu
To talk to the turtle
Till ten to two.

*S*pades for the circling turrets,
Clubs for the towers above,
Diamonds for sparkling windows,
And Hearts for love.

*T*he bewitching winds come
They whistle and thrum
The Wind-Witch is wild as the night.

Her cold, flashing stare
Loosens gales from her hair
Entangling the creatures in flight.

Winds whirl up the coast
Town and country are tossed
Till the storm blows out to the sea.

In my loom's warp and woof
Thimbles bound in blue stuff
Flashing lights on the woods' tapestry.

A patch of blue
Is memory's dawn,
A page in the sky
From which I have drawn.

My dream trolley's wheels
Shower sparks to the ground,
And grind to a halt
As the children hop down.

We've circled back home
From the start to the end –
I took the first turn
Now it's your turn, my friend.

Skip Aboard
Children

Hurry if you can
Trolley's now leaving
For Thimbledon land
It won't cost a penny
It won't cost a dime
All in together now
We leave on time.
We'll rock on the bridge
Along Trolley Line Lane,
We'll fish, stitch and picnic
And dance in the rain.

Thimbledon

Out of the blue

THIMBLEDON BRIDGE IS A MERRY MILE LONG. NO ONE CAN CROSS WHO IS CROSS

THIMBLEDON BRIDGE

SEW A STITCH — CAST A LINE — CATCH YOUR FISH — AND
I'LL CATCH MINE

MY CLOTH WORKS MAGIC

SINK THE NEEDLE INTO THE BLUE
DRAW OUT RABBITS — BABY-DOE, TOO.

AND LIKE A POOL

REFLECTS ALL

STORIES IN MY HEAD

WHO'S AFRAID OF VIRGINIA'S WOOF

FISHES IN MY PAIL

ONE STITCH.
TWO STITCH.
CATCH 'EM BY THE TAIL

SEEK NO FURTHER
MARRY ME
MEANDERING MAID
IN MY APPLE TREE.

IMAGES REELED FROM MY SPOOL

I SEW OLD TALES

I THINK I KNOW
JUST WHERE WE ARE
WE'RE HALF-WAY UNDER
THE MORNING STAR

The ANTELOPE

ROLL ALONG TROLLEY DING, RING THE BELL, DONG! HERE'S ANTELOPE STATION IS EVERY ONE ON?

THE JOURNEY'S AS SILENT AS SNOWFALLS AT NIGHT. FOLKS THINK WE'RE NEARBY BUT WE'VE SLIPPED OUT OF SIGHT WE'VE SLIPPED OUT OF SIGHT out of sight

ONE FOR THE MONEY
TWO FOR THE SHOW
TEDDY SINGS "READY!"
GOAT CRIES GO!

WE TRANSFER BY FERRY ROUND RIDE-A-WAY PLACE WHERE WEE-MOUSE AND LONG-HARE GET SET FOR A RACE.

WINDS BLOW EAST
WINDS BLOW WEST
BRANCHES TANGLE
BILLOWS CREST

CAT'S AT THE WINDOW
OSTRICH IN THE GLADE
ELEPHANT AND ZEBRA
GIRAFFE PARADE

MUFFIN

TIGER TIPTOES TO TIMBUCTU TO TALK TO THE TURTLE TILL TEN TO TWO

THE BEWITCHING WINDS COME
THEY WHISTLE AND THRUM
THE WIND WITCH IS WILD AS
THE NIGHT

HER COLD FLASHING STARE LOOSENS GALES FROM HER HAIR ENTANGLING THE CREATURES IN FLIGHT

TOWN AND COUNTRY ARE TOSSED TILL THE STORM BLOWS OUT TO THE SEA

IN MY LOOM'S WARP AND WOOF
THIMBLES BOUND IN BLUE STUFF
FLASHING LIGHTS ON THE WOODS TAPESTRY

A PATCH OF BLUE
IS MEMORY'S DAWN
A PAGE IN THE SKY
FROM WHICH I HAVE
DRAWN.

My dream trolley's wheels
Shower sparks to the ground
And grind to a halt
As the children hop down.

We've circled back home
From the start to the end.
I took the first turn
Now it's your turn, my friend.

Marvin Bileck's life (March 2, 1920–April 29, 2005) was spent as an artist, as an educator, and as a designer and illustrator of children's books. His titles include *Sugarplum*, *Penny*, and *A Walker in the City* by Alfred Kazan. His exquisitely detailed drawings for *Rain Makes Applesauce* have helped to make it a children's classic and a Caldecott Honor book.

Bileck and his wife, Emily Nelligan, lived and worked as artists on Great Cranberry Island, Maine and in Winsted, Connecticut where Emily still resides.

Photo: Emily Nelligan

Author, artist and teacher Ashley Bryan has been a leading figure in children's literature for over 50 years. In 1962, he was the first African American man to both write and illustrate a book for children. His work has earned numerous honors including the Virginia Hamilton and the Arbuthnot Awards for lifetime achievement, the Regina Medal, the Laura Ingalls Wilder Award and several Coretta Scott King awards and honors, as well as being named a New York Public Library Literary Lion.

Ashley Bryan lives on Little Cranberry Island (Islesford) off the coast of Maine where the elementary school is named in his honor and where, in the summer of 2014, the Islesford Historical Museum held the first exhibition of the Ashley Bryan Center. www.ashleybryancenter.org

Library of Congress Control Number: 2014951309
ISBN 978-0-9793000-4-2

Design and production by Julie Allred and Beth Mauldin, BW&A Books, Inc.
Digital scans of Marvin Bileck's original art courtesy of Alexandre Gallery www.alexandregallery.com
First printing. Printed in China.
Production Location: Guangdong, China
Production Date: 12/1/2014
Cohort: Batch 1

www.alazar-press.com

Alazar
PRESS